CW00840171

DIARY

of a

Legendary
Ender Dragon

VOLUME 1

Christopher Craft

Welcome To Another Awesome Adventure!

Steve has decided that he's done everything that there is to do in Minecraft, and now he's looking for adventure. Little did he know that adventure was also looking for him! When Steve finds the journal of the Legendary Ender Dragon, he finds out that it takes more than just brute strength to be the Ender Dragon, and it takes more than just courage to become a legend. Join Steve, Morach, Dagger, and Flip in the adventure of a lifetime, full of action, adventure, and friendship.

An exciting set of engaging tales, suitable for kids and adults alike!

Fiction Disclaimer

This is a work of fiction. Names, characters, businesses, places, events and incidents are either the products of the author's imagination or used in a fictitious manner. Any resemblance to actual persons, living or dead, or actual events is purely coincidental.

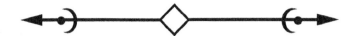

Table of Contents

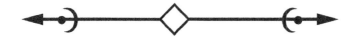

Chapter 1:

STEVE THE BORED EXPLORER

STEVE HAD BEEN WANDERING AROUND AIMLESSLY for a while now, and honestly, it wasn't nearly as interesting as he'd hoped it would be. Sure the all night battle royal between him and the monsters that spawned from the darkness weren't dull, but after a while they became more of a chore than an opportunity. Steve was reaching a point in his adventuring career where nothing really took him by surprise anymore. He'd seen all the sea temples, underground caverns, and portals to the Nether that he'd wanted to see, and now he was just a traveler without a destination.

Even still, Steve was happy to be where he was at in life. He had five stacks of cooked steak, fully enchanted diamond gear, and a map that was nearly filled. Oh yes, the map. Steve had adventures all over his Minecraft world, but in the back of his mind he always knew he was avoiding that one place; the dark zone.

See, when Steve was still a newbie and barely knew how to open his inventory, he had spawned in the dark zone. It was a forest filled with oak trees, and it rained there all the time. Even in the middle of the day, monsters would spawn randomly, and in groups. Steve hadn't even made his first crafting table before he'd been blown up by a creeper and shot down by skeletons. And who could forget the spiders? Just thinking about their beady red eyes and sharp teeth made the hair of Steve's neck stand on end. Basically, the dark zone was the most dangerous land in the entire world of Minecraft, and it was also the next stop on Steve's list.

Steve looked down at his map. He was directly in front of the beige blank spot. He looked up at the usually blue sky and saw that it was now gray and dark. He held out his hand and felt the beginnings of rain. He took a deep breath to calm his nerves, and then started walking, suddenly missing the boring life of a traveler. He walked farther and farther on until the missing piece of the map was completely revealed. It was now raining ocelots and wolves, so he ran over to a nearby tree for shelter from the rain. He then built a two block high wall around himself, and threw torches down on every surface. He wasn't going to be ambushed in here, no sir.

"Oh, what's this then?" Steve said, looking down at a strange dark spot on the map. It was small but noticeable, if only because it was doing something Steve had never seen on the map; the dark spot was moving. It seemed to be moving incredibly fast, and it didn't even slow down for hills or even mountains. Steve was in complete shock. Before he could get his wits about him, he noticed that the dark spot was coming towards him, and fast. Before Steve could decide if it was better to build a roof and be protected or leave it open and see the creature, it was already over him.

Whatever it was, it was big, bigger than any other living thing Steve had ever come across, including ghosts. It had wings like a bat, but even seeing such a huge creature soar through the air that easily was hard to believe. Steve blinked his eyes a few times to make sure he was really seeing what he was seeing. Sooner than he'd hoped though, the creature was gone, and the forest seemed unnaturally still. Steve took another look down at the map, and saw the very last trace of the creature disappear.

"It went underground." Steve said aloud to himself. Steve could feel his heart beat in his chest as something dawned on him. This was the thing he had been looking for without even realizing it. His final adventure would be one for the history books.

Steve made a mental note of where exactly the creature disappeared, then tore down his walls and sprinted through the rainy forest. After running for a while, he looked down and checked the map again. He was at the right spot, but for some reason, there were no crevices or ravines for him to climb down. A creature of that size couldn't have just vanished into thin air; Steve knew that, so he kept searching.

After an embarrassingly long search, Steve decided he'd found the creature's hiding spot. He crossed a river, thinking that the mountain on the other side would be it, but was instead surprised to find that the river had no bottom. From either side of the river, it seemed normal enough, but from a bird's eye view, it was obvious that this was where the creature was hiding away.

Steve took a deep breath and dove down, kicking his legs wildly and flailing his arms like a mad man. Somehow his diamond armor didn't make him sink any faster, so all he could do was wait to reach the bottom of what was apparently the world's largest cascading waterfall. By the time he could see through the dark murky water enough to make out the opening of a tunnel, Steve was out of air. Every second of wait time meant more and more hearts gone. If Steve looked like a weirdo with his kicking and splashing at the surface, he looked insane right now. His face was turning blue, and he only had three hearts left when he finally managed to get a gasp of fresh air. He jumped out of the water and into a cavern, flopping like a fish.

"Next time, I'll just tie a rock to my boots and hope for the best." Steve said to himself, finally standing up and taking a look around. There were torches along the left wall all the way down the

cavern as far as Steve could see. It didn't seem to be manmade, but he still felt like it was familiar. "I've come this far, no sense in turning back now." Steve said. And with that, he was off.

The cavern wasn't very big, only about five

blocks at its widest and four blocks at its tallest. Actually, Steve was beginning to feel a little cramped and claustrophobic, but tried to keep that out of his mind, which was hard, considering he sweat a lot when he was nervous. By the time he actually saw the end of the cavern, Steve's boots were making a squishy noise with each step, like he'd just taken another dip in the river. He did a quick sniff of his pits before meeting his destiny. He really needed to find the crafting recipe for deodorant.

Pushing that from his mind, Steve continued on. At the end of the cavern was a library. It had two floors, each surrounded with a perimeter of book shelves. Steve was on the first floor, and when he looked up, he had to squint against the light of the chandelier. Once his eyes adjusted, he was able to take an even closer look around. It was then that his heart sunk. His luck with voiding monsters was about to run out.

Spider webs covered nearly every flat surface in the library, and considering everything was made of cubes, that was a lot. Steve pulled out his diamond sword and started walking onward, throwing down torches everywhere, even if it was only a bit shady. He walked between the book shelves, but even the isles that the maze of shelves created was filled to the brim with sticky spider silk. Luckily, as long as Steve didn't touch any of it, his sword would eat through it like a hot knife slices through butter.

"Yummy, butter..." Steve said absentmindedly, when all of the sudden, his stomach roared louder than any zombie ever had. He checked his hunger, and saw that he was almost starved. He decided a lunch break was in order, and so he sheathed his sword and pulled out some juicy steaks from his inventory. Steve preferred chicken, but he was so hungry he would have eaten dirt and not the fancy tilled, earthy kind either. The weird light brown kind that you find a thousand miles under ground.

After the first three huge steaks, Steve knew the pressure was on to pace himself so as to keep his cubic figure intact, so he just nibbled on the last one before wiping the remains from his mouth and standing up. His diamond armor seemed to fit a little tighter than it had before he sat down. Steve burped loudly, and then pulled his diamond sword out again just in time.

An arrow soared through the air and gave Steve a hard smack to the back of the head. If it hadn't been for his helmet, Steve would be a kabob right about then.

"Alright, who's the wise guy?" Steve said, spinning on his heel to face his attacker. It was a skeletal archer, a creature with sunken black eyes and a decent aim. But Steve couldn't focus on the skeleton when he looked lower and noticed what the skeleton was riding. Sure enough, there was a spider, looking perfectly content while standing in a web, holding the skeleton just above it. Steve looked at each one of its red eyes and decided that the best course of action was a prompt retreat.

Apparently, there was a party in the library and the only people invited were spiders, because just as soon as Steve turned to run, he was face to face with a conga line of the evil looking beasts. Being the hero that he was, Steve chose to face his foe, but being the person of average intelligence that he was, he decided a fight with one spider was better than a fight with five, so he turned back around as quickly as he could, and brought his sword up into striking position. Even though he was feeling a little less than courageous, Steve decided to let out his war screech as he charged at the skeletal archer and his little spider friend.

"Oh yeah, you're going to get it now!" Steve shouted, and his roar echoed through the underground library. He took about three steps, and then realized something was off. He had his eyes clinched shut, and when he opened them, he realized he wasn't moving. The longer he stood there, the more he realized something worse; he was sinking.

Steve looked down and saw that he had fallen into a spider trap, a two block deep, and one block wide hole filled with spider webs. He couldn't jump, and he was moving so slowly he might as well be standing still. Steve looked behind himself and saw a barrage of arrows fly in his direction. He did his best to duck out of the way, but most of them sprayed against the back of his diamond armor. He lost about three hearts, nothing major, but he didn't want to take too many more hits like that. In front of him was the spider riding skeletal archer, bow primed and ready to fire. Steve braced himself for impact, but was relieved when he hadn't been hit. Steve stopped cringing long enough to open his eyes, and started panicking when he saw that the reason the skeleton had missed was because the spider was charging towards him!

"Not good, not good, not good!" Steve shouted. He pulled out his bow and arrow, and tried taking a few shots, but he kept missing because of his shaky, terrified hands. Instead, Steve pulled his sword back out and started hacking and slashing at the web he was in, hoping not to whack off his legs in the process. It was slow going, and he was getting pelted from behind and charged at from the front. He was at five hearts by the time the spider reached him, but luckily that was the moment that the bottom piece of web broke. Unfortunately for Steve, there wasn't anything underneath.

Steve kept falling and falling down the dark cave shaft, screaming at the top of his lungs as he

fell. He smacked the ground hard, nearly breaking his legs in the process. Although Steve would never admit it, he did pee a little.

"How am I not dead?" Steve said out loud. He was feeling a bit tipsy, and so he looked at his heart bar. He was sitting pretty at exactly half of a heart. Half of a heart left! As if to prove Steve wrong, an arrow came flying down from the top of the hole. The skeletons really didn't like to lose.

Stick pulled out a dirt block and plugged the hole just as the arrow smashed into it. He heard the arrow crack, and felt relieved that the crack had been the stick it was made out of and not his own forehead.

"This giant monster better be here or so help me..." Steve grumbled to himself as he patted the dust from his now filthy looking diamond armor. When he finally got his wits about him, Steve looked up and saw that there was yet another chandelier, just like the one upstairs. In the center of the room was a podium.

Steve walked over to the podium. On it was a book, open to the middle page. "I know this looks good, but who in the world reads a book from the middle?" Steve said confusedly. Disregarding that, he closed the book to look at the front cover. It had a jewel encrusted image of the creature he had seen!

"Diary of the Legendary Ender Dragon...

wow!" Steve shouted. So it was the Ender Dragon! The creature of myth and legend, the creature that guarded the End and here was its diary! "I bet I could get the inside scoop on how to take it down!" Steve said to himself. The diary was basically a cheat sheet for the battle ahead. Steve knew where the dragon was, and now he would know how to win. Now all he had to do was... read it.

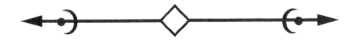

Chapter 2:

THE NOT SO LEGENDARY
ENDER DRAGON

IT WAS THE BEGINNING OF THE EXAM, AND I WAS... well, I was a little less than prepared. My opponent was Garon, a lava dragon. He could spit fireballs from his mouth, and his scales were a thousand degrees. Basically what I'm trying to say is, things were not looking so good for me.

"Alright students. This is the last round of training before the games. As you know, this is just basic sparring, so if the other person taps out, the fight is over, okay? We don't want anyone getting hurt before the games begin."

the teacher said, flapping her wings as she spoke. She was my favorite teacher, but she taught my worst subject, combat. Well, that is if you don't count flying... or stealth, or any of the other courses offered. What can I say; I'm a lover not a fighter.

"Time to fight, kid." She said as reality sunk in and I realized I couldn't love my way out of this one. I stepped up to a large circular ring on the floor. There were two lines, and I took my place on the line closest to me. On the other line facing me was Garon.

"Guess what Morach? When I'm done with you, you'll be crying to your momma. Oh yeah, get ready to feel the burn!" Garon said, spitting a little as he spoke. He smiled like he was clever, and I tried not to roll my eyes even though every cell in my body wanted to. Sadly, even though Garon was a rude jerk, he was also one of the best fighters out of the group, and like I said before, I am not. My plan was to try not to offend him, and tap out as soon as possible. I was useless, but I wasn't an idiot. At least I had that going for me.

"All right, are you both ready?" the teacher

said. I gave her a nervous nod, and Garon just sort of growled in her general direction. Geez, the guy didn't even know if he was a dragon or a dog. "Then on the count of three, start your match. 3... 2... 1... FIGHT!" She shouted, and I instantly swung my tail to the ground to tap out. Sadly though, Garon beat me to the draw and was already tackling me to the ground.

He hooked his claws around me and wouldn't let go. I felt like I was in an oven, and my scales were starting to smell like a well done steak; not a good sign. I used my tail and wedged it between his hands and my back and used it like a crowbar to separate us. He jumped back and landed lightly on his feet, and I scrambled up onto mine and spun around to face him. He opened his mouth and I could see the flames building in the back of his throat. If I knew how, this would be the time for me to charge my own attack, but sadly, I wasn't much of a dragon, and so I did the only thing I knew how to do; I tapped out, and this time, it worked.

"Oh, come on! We were just getting to the good part!" Garon whined at the teacher. She just looked at him with a furrowed brow and frowned.

"If Morach doesn't want to continue, then he shouldn't have to continue. It's that simple. Let it go Garon." She snapped at him. I was happy that someone would stick up for me, but she was doing more harm than good, because now Garon was angry, and he'd want to take it out on someone after class.

"Alright students, gather round. As you all know, the Games are upon us. You will be the first dragons in one thousand years to fight for your chance to become the new Ender Dragon. I'm sure by now you're bored to death of all the details, so I'll let you go to your nests and rest up for tomorrow, but I do have a word of advice. These challenges are going to be more dangerous than they've even been before. If you have any doubts whatsoever, maybe it is best that you do not participate. Anyway, now that I've scared you all half to death... sweet dreams!" the teacher said, bounding upwards and flying off o her nest. Usually after class is over, everyone groups together and talks or gossips, but today was different. It was hard to be nice to someone when you knew they would be your enemy the very next day. Luckily, I didn't have that problem because I didn't have any friends in the first place. No one wants to be friends with a dragon who can't even do anything that a dragon is supposed to do. Yep, I can't breathe fire or fly. As I watched all the other students fly away from the training arena and towards the woods where our nests were, I couldn't help but feel a little bit like I shouldn't even enter the Games. I mean, what chance did I have?

I figured I might as well not worry about it till tomorrow, because I had a long walk home. My nest just happened to be one of the farthest away from, well, everything. Since I couldn't fly, I always had to walk home, but it wasn't all bad. In fact, sometimes I really liked being able to just be with nature and take it all in.

Today was not one of those times though, sadly. I just wanted to be home and in my nest. I hurried up and started running instead of walking. By the time I was halfway to my nest, I was ready to drop.

"Alright Dagger, time to pay up. I know you have your Redstone piece on you, and I want it. So hand it over!" Said a voice. Of course, even though the voice was coming from a good distance away I instantly knew who it belonged to. Garon was up to his bullying ways again. I

crept over as quietly as I could so I could scope out the scene.

"Garon, come on, you know we need them to enter the Games. You have yours, why can't you just leave mine alone?" Said a voice I also recognized. It was Dagger, the only other dragon to have as low marks as me even though he can fly and breathe fire. It was just like Garon to pick on someone weaker than he was.

I finally got within view of the struggle, and it didn't look too good for Dagger. Garon had him pinned down, and Dagger was a zombie dragon, he wasn't strong enough to throw Garon off. I knew I couldn't take Garon down by myself. Even if I had Dagger helping me, the odds were not in our favor, and if I stepped in and lost, it'd be my Redstone that Garon would take.

I hated that I was powerless, that I couldn't do anything to help. I had no abilities, and I didn't even know what kind of dragon I was. Some of the teachers even said that I might not be a dragon at all! But it still wasn't fair. Garon shouldn't be able to push people around and steal their chance at greatness, no matter how small they were. As I thought about it, I got angrier and angrier. I felt fire ignite in my belly. I had to be a warrior, I had to stand up to bullies and help those in need. I couldn't just stand around and do nothing! The passionate I felt, the more powerful I felt, until eventually, I couldn't take it anymore. I jumped out from the cover of the forest.

"Garon, walk away now, and we can forget this ever happened." I said, hoping Garon would just leave peacefully. He looked surprised, and it took him a second to recognize me, but when he did, he smiled like I'd said something funny.

"Oh whatever, you and what army? You couldn't even fight me in the ring, what are you going to do? You know what? I'm going to take your Redstone too! You don't deserve to compete in the Games!" Garon shouted. He jumped off of Dagger and started charging at me. I knew I was probably a goner, but something told me to just stand my ground.

Dagger had jumped up and started charging a fireball. When he finally fired, the aim was perfect, but Garon expected it. With one swing of his tail, Garon knocked the fireball away like it was nothing, not even turning to look. Dagger had given it his best shot, but it looked like I was on my own. I opened my mouth to shout just before Garon would have crashed into me, but instead of a shot, something else came out. A fireball.

When it launched, I could feel a burning sensation in the back of my throat. It flew at Garon so fast that I could barely see it fly, but when it collided with him, there was a loud boom like an explosion. Garon was knocked right on his butt, and he looked up like he couldn't believe what had just happened. Honestly, I was having trouble believing it myself.

"I'll get you back for that Morach!" Garon shouted as he scrambled up and then started flapping his wings. In no time he was in the air, probably heading straight for his nest. He would probably be out to get me in the Games, but I couldn't even think about that. I had breathed fire for the first time! I was officially a fire breathing dragon!

"Wow Morach, I had no idea you could do that! I had always heard you couldn't breathe fire, but that was some of the best I've ever seen!" Dagger said, running towards me. I was smiling from ear to ear, and didn't know quite how to respond. "I mean, did you see Garon's face? I

thought he was going to explode! You've got to teach me how to do that. My name's Dagger, by the way. Thanks for... well, saving me." Dagger said. He seemed like kind of a scatter brain, but he was nice enough.

"Actually, I'm not really sure how I did that, it kind of just happened." I said honestly. Whatever that was, it wasn't on purpose. I had no idea how to just do it again.

"Oh, I see. Saving all your secret moves for the Games? Hey, I can respect that. But I'll warn you, I'm vicious! Everyone knows the last Ender dragon was a zombie dragon, so I'm sure to win. If you want to team up with me though, I'd let you tag along." Dagger said, while stumbling over his own legs, trying to show off some odd fighting style that kind of looked like he had to go to the bathroom.

"I'll take you up on that offer. Everyone else is planning to form groups in the Games, I guess this is ours." I said. Dagger wasn't that powerful, but neither was I except for that one fireball, and if I couldn't do it again, then I had exactly zero chance of winning the Games. At least this way, we could both have a fighting chance.

"Awesome! We'll call ourselves Team Ender! Listen, I've got to go though. I think I left my milk out, and I want to go drink it before it spoils... you know, more than it already is. See ya! Go Team

Ender!" Dagger said happily as he took off. The guy was a ball of hyperactivity, which is weird for a zombie dragon on account of the fact that they're, well, zombies.

I walked the rest of the way home with a grin. I had tried making another fireball, and while I could never get them as big or as explosive as the one I sent at Garon, they were still enough for combat. I might actually stand a chance. Unless they required that we fly five blocks in front of us, in which case, I might be sunk, but I tried to remain positive. I was in an alliance, and what's even better still is the fact that I think I made a friend. I might not be the most capable dragon, but at least I wasn't alone.

By the time I reached my nest, it was already dark outside. The stars had come out, and the moon was high in the sky. I was exhausted, but even then I was so excited that it took a while to fall asleep.

"Morach the Legendary Ender Dragon, I like the sound of that." I said to myself, just before I fell asleep. I dreamed of winning the Games, being crowned the Ender dragon, and finally being able to get the respect I deserve.

As far as I was concerned, tomorrow couldn't come fast enough, and that was a great feeling. Better than pie? I wouldn't go that far, but still pretty great.

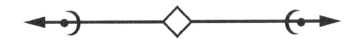

Chapter 3:

LET THE GAMES BEGIN

"**M**ORACH, WAKE UP! IT'S BEEN DAYLIGHT FOR like, ten minutes! Get up, lazy bones!" Dagger shouted from just outside my door. If friendship meant having him wake me up three hours early for everything, I don't know that I wanted it.

"Okay, okay, geez." I said. I stretched, rubbed the remaining sleep from my eyes, and then took a little dip in the tub to get my scales nice and shiny. I was a solid black dragon with purple features, so dirt didn't really stand out that much on me, but I liked to be clean anyway. If I was going to be the Legendary Ender Dragon, I'd need to smell like one. I dried off quickly, and then made my way outside.

"Sorry for waking you up so early, but come on! This is the first day of the Games, how were you even able to sleep? I know I didn't get any." Dagger said, smiling.

We made our way past the training grounds, and then had to walk onward to the arena where the portals to each of the games were held. Dagger could have flown and made it there in just a few minutes, but since he was walking with me, it took us close to an hour. Still, Dagger didn't seem to be mad about it, and I was thankful for that.

When we arrived, the place was packed. I couldn't believe it. It had been an hour, maybe an hour and a half since sunrise, and the teacher said that the sign ups didn't even start until noon! "I think they all came sometime last night. I must not have been the only one too nervous to get some sleep." Dagger said. He was right.

We walked together to the back of the line, and waited until the sun reached the middle of the sky. Then the teacher took her place at the

front of the portal gates and started explaining what was happening. The Games were about to begin!

"Alright, students. I know all of you have been hearing about the three trials since you first began your training, but we have to go over them one more time, as is tradition. Today begins the first challenge, the Maze. All of you will be placed in teams of three. You may choose your partners, but if you don't have any, that's fine too. Any group that is missing one or more of their partners will be assigned the remaining partners at random. So, everyone, get in your groups." She said, and immediately after she finished, everyone began swarming around, trying to find partners. Dagger and I just stood where we were, hoping that one of the stronger dragons would want to join our team, but none of them did. We would have to get a random partner.

I turned and saw that Garon, however, was choosing his team from a group. He might have been a bully, but it was better to be on his team than have to go up against him. Of course, in the end, Garon chose the two strongest looking people, who were both creeper dragons. They were bright green with beady black eyes. Most definitely not the sort of dragons I'd want on my team. Plus, they tend to explode over every little thing, so there's that. When Garon finally saw

Dagger and me standing off to the side of the crowds, he pointed and made a thumbs down. I guess he was still pretty ticked off. I made a mental note to avoid him at all costs.

"Without further ado, I'd like to present you with your challenge. Once you enter the portal, you will be teleported to a random point in the maze. In addition to having to find the exit, you will have to survive. If you are defeated in battle, or if you fall into a trap, you will be transported back and that will be the end of the competition for you. There will be several chests with golden apples. You will use them to regain health. In one random chest, there will be a surprise. Whoever finds it will have an advantage. The exit door will open at the end of day three, and you will have one hour to make it out. Oh, and one more thing... you can't use your wings. Good luck everyone." The teacher said.

After that, we all started making our way towards the gate that guarded the portal. Since there were so many of us, there were two lines, and two portals to the Maze. Dagger and I were towards the back of the line, so we had the

longest time to wait. Once we reached the front, we had a teacher ask us for out Redstone. When I gave them my piece, I looked over and saw Garon hand over three pieces. The teacher looked confused, but let him go on anyway. I couldn't believe he would do that. Dagger and I were shuffled forward until we were in front of the portal. As smiley as Dagger had been this morning, he looked nervous. I tried to smile to reassure him, but I don't know if it was very convincing, because honestly, I was nervous too. I took a deep breath, and walked forward. The portal was glowing blue, and when I walked inside it, that's all I could see. Then, everything started to wobble and spin until I felt dizzy. I closed my eyes to try and block it out, and then when I opened them, I was there, in the Maze.

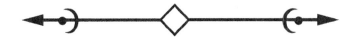

Chapter 4:

THE GOOD, THE BAD,
AND THE SLIME

THE MAZE WASN'T EXACTLY HOW I PICTURED IT. The walls were made of gray stone, and the ceiling was made of glass. Everything was incredibly close together and low. I looked to my left and saw Dagger, and he was facing me, but he wasn't looking at me. Instead he was looking behind me. I turned and saw our third partner. He wasn't exactly how I pictured him either.

He was a slime dragon, and an odd one at that. His scales were a dark shade of green, and he looked like he was covered in an ooze of some sort. His eyes were perfectly round, and honestly, he kind of gave me the creeps, but I didn't say anything. We would be partners for the next three days, and I wanted to make a good first impression.

"Hi, my name is Morach. What's yours?" I said, trying my best to smile and be polite. The slime dragon just sort of stared at me, and I tried to pretend it wasn't weird. Sadly, Dagger wasn't as thoughtful or as tactful, and he just cut right to the heart of the matter.

"Wow, you're freaky looking. I mean, there's nothing wrong with that, but wow." Dagger said. Instead of being offended, the slime dragon just stared a bit longer with his round, wide eyes. Then he finally said something.

"Flip is my name. Let's go!" He said, still smiling and still staring. At the very least, he didn't seem offended, and he was right; we needed to go.

"Alright you guys, we need to find the exit. The teacher said that it would open up after three days, and we'd only have an hour to get through, so we have to find the exit and then wait there until it opens. Agreed?" I said, trying to get the team mobilized. Everyone else was probably already making their way towards the exit, and we'd spent the first ten minutes just getting to know each other. Not a good start, to say the least.

"Agreed!" Dagger said enthusiastically. Flip didn't say anything, but it was his idea, so I figured that meant that he agreed. So we were fifteen minutes into the Maze, and we finally started walking.

We had spawned in a dead end. In front of us was a two way path. We could go left, or we could go right. I was taking the lead, so I chose to go left. I could hear Dagger's footsteps right behind me I walked on, but then I heard a squishing noise heading away from me. I turned and saw that Flip decided to go right. I looked at Dagger, and he had the same look on his face that I did. There was no use arguing with Flip, and I had a feeling he would just go the direction he wanted to go anyway, so Dagger nodded to me, and we just followed behind Flip.

We did this for a long time, just taking

random turns and seeing where they went. We came across a few dead ends, but we had yet to come across a chest. All the while, Flip was basically leading the way. He never said a word, and when he started going in circles, Dagger finally decided to speak up.

"Listen Flip, I'm fine with you choosing the route, it's basically random anyway, but I swear we've passed this same corridor three times already. Can't you just let one of us take the lead for a little bit?" Dagger asked. Flip just gave him that same wide eyes stare, then shook his head and walked on. It was hopeless. Dagger and I just sighed and continued on. Even if we weren't finding anything of value, at least we weren't being attacked. Maybe that's why Flip had us going in circles... I doubted it, but it was the only thing that was keeping Dagger and me from ditching him at that point.

Eventually, I looked up and through the glass ceiling and saw that the sun was beginning to fall down over the horizon. It was going to be night time soon, and we had an important decision to make. Did we try and get some sleep so we'd be fully rested for the next day, or did we stay up all night and continue going through the maze while most of the other teams were sleeping? We followed Flip until the only source of light was the moon and we could barely see our own tales. He walked down a hall that was, of course,

another dead end. But this time, there was something there!

I ran ahead of Dagger who was already yawning from sleepiness, and then came upon the small brown box. Flip stepped aside, and I pulled up on the lid, revealing a whole mess of glowing golden apples! There were at least a dozen sitting in rows of four at the bottom of the chest. I handed one to Dagger and then another to Flip before grabbing one for myself. We all started chowing down on them, and let me just say, they are the greatest food in the world. There were perfectly juicy, and perfectly sweet. When we finished eating, out health and hunger bars were full. For once, we all looked at each other and smiled happily, Flip included. I reached in to grab the remaining apples so we could put them in our inventory, but before I even got close, Flip stepped between me and the chest.

"Hey, what gives?" I said. Those apples were the only thing we had to bring up our health, and since we were a team, we couldn't afford to be greedy. For the first time since we set off through the maze, Flip spoke up.

"We should leave them in the chest. If we get ambushed in the night and one of us is eliminated, then we won't lose any apples like we would if they were in their inventory." He said with an odd look on his face. The way he was

acting all day, I still didn't know if I could trust him, but what he said made sense. I looked over at Dagger for approval, and he nodded, again yawning while he did.

"Does this mean we get to sleep here for the

night? Because if I have to walk down one more dead end before I get my beauty rest, I'm going to blow a fuse. Who's with me?" Dagger said, and we both nodded our approval. We were all tired from walking, and the only way we'd be any use in the competition the next day would be if we got a good night's sleep.

We all lay down, and almost immediately Dagger was snoring. It was so loud that I was genuinely afraid that he'd give away out location. I had to whack him with my tail a few times so he would be quiet, but finally he started sleeping quietly, and I fell asleep too. I didn't wake up the entire night, but when Dagger and I finally got up to start the day, we were alone.

"Where did Flip go?" I asked while doing a long morning stretch. Dagger rubbed his eyes, and then took a look around. He wasn't anywhere along the path we had taken. We both gave each other a look of worry, and I jumped up as quickly as I could and ran over to the chest.

"I knew it! He stole all the golden apples!" I shouted, maybe a little louder than I should have. Still, I was angry. We trusted him, and this is how

he repaid us. Boy, did we feel like chumps.

"I felt a bad vibe coming off of him since we stepped through that portal. If he wanted to compete on his own, we could have given him his share of apples and everything would be fine, but no. He had to go be a jerk about it!" Dagger said, fuming as well.

Since there was nothing we could actually do about it, we decided in the end to just let it go. Besides, now that he was gone, the team was probably better off. At the very least, we'd stop going in circles.

This time, Dagger took the lead, and he was a pretty good navigator. As far as I could tell, we never ended up in the same place twice, but even still, we weren't finding anything. When we did finally come across something, I kind of wished we hadn't.

"Dagger, look over there." I said quietly, hungering down and trying to make myself look less visible. Down one of the paths that led to a dead end, on the stone wall, there were scorch marks. Someone had shot a fireball at the wall. One of the rules of the Maze was that if you broke something like the stone or glass, you were automatically disqualified, so the only other alternative became clear. They didn't shoot the fireball to destroy the wall; they shot it to destroy another dragon.

"Morach, we need to get out of here. It's only the second day, and someone's picking fights. Besides, look at those scorch marks. The only dragon with fire hot enough to leave those is..." Dagger whispered, trailing off. I just looked at him and nodded. Garon had been here. Only a lava dragon could have done this, and only Garon would be bold enough to take on another team on the second day.

Dagger and I ran quickly and stealthily towards the scorch marks so we could get a better look. Dagger reached out and touched them, but quickly jumped back.

"Ouch! They're still hot. That means Garon's close by. We need to get out of here, Morach." Dagger said, and I couldn't agree more. Garon was very clear that if we met each other in the competition, he's do everything in his power to get us out. The first challenge was made so that it would thing out the herd down to a fourth of what it started out as. In order to get through it, you needed to keep your head down and just go.

So Dagger and I did just that. We started making our way through the maze as quickly as possible, while also checking over our shoulders every time we made a turn. We were both glad we got some sleep because we weren't even halfway through the day and we were exhausted. Being paranoid was tiresome work.

We sat down to rest, but only had a moment before we heard a low rumbling noise. It seemed to come from the other side of one of the walls. Dagger and I put our ears to the wall and listened to see if we could hear it again. We waited for just a moment longer, and then another boom resounded, shaking the wall and floor. I had a feeling it would be Garon, and something was unsettling about that. If he lost all of his health, he'd lose his chance at becoming the Ender dragon. So if he was willing to make that much noise, and leave a trail of scorch marks behind, he must be confident, too confident. Garon had a huge ego, but even he wouldn't risk losing at this stage in the competition.

"Morach, I say we get out of here. I'm at less than half hunger, which means we can't regenerate our health if we get into a fight. Even if we somehow managed to defeat Garon and

those creeper dragons he's teamed up with, we'd just be easy targets for whatever group found us first." Dagger said with his ear against the wall, waiting for another boom to tell us where Garon was. Then another one resounded, but this one was closer, much closer.

"Alright, he's heading our way, so we need to keep going ahead, and then stay to the left. If we can find just one chest, we'll be golden." I said, and with that, we both started sprinting down the path, Dagger looking behind us and me in front of us. The booms started coming from behind us, meaning that Garon was somewhere back where the original scorch marks were. We started making random turns to the left until we were confident we were as far away from him as possible. We looked up, and the sun was going down once again.

"Morach, do you think we should stop? I mean, we haven't heard anything for a while now, and we could use the rest. Tomorrow we have to find the exit gate." Dagger said, just as we rounded a corner and ended up at a dead end for the millionth time. I looked at him and realized how tired he was, and then realized how tired I was too. We'd be useless tomorrow if we didn't get at least a little rest.

"Why don't we take turns standing watch, that way if someone tries to sneak up on us, we'll be able to wake up in time to defend ourselves?"

Dagger nodded and then yawned. "I'll take the first watch. You get some shut eye, you've earned it." I said, and Dagger smiled, then walked slowly to a corner and curled up. In a matter of seconds, he was out like a Redstone lamp.

I started pacing back and forth, trying to stay awake. After about an hour of that, I sat down. It had been completely silent since the first explosions, and so I started thinking that I could just rest. Maybe it wasn't even Garon at all. Maybe there was a group of dragons who found him and eliminated him from the competition, and that's what all the exploding was about. But then again, maybe it was him, and maybe the explosions were because of the secret item that the teacher had mentioned. Whatever it was, she said that it would give the dragon who found it an advantage in the maze. Being able to blow up your enemies definitely sounded like an advantage to me. Sadly, if that were true, that meant that Garon would be nearly unstoppable.

I tried thinking of other things, but I always ended up coming back to sheep, and that wasn't helping me stay awake as much as it sounds. It took every ounce of willpower not to close my eyes, and then I heard something that jolted me awake. It was an explosion, and it was close.

"Dagger, get up, I think Garon's on his way!" I whispered to Dagger, and he did get up, but at a lot slower pace than I would have liked. He started rubbing his eyes and yawning, but then we heard another, even louder explosion, and this time it sounded like it was even closer than before. That woke Dagger right up. We started running toward the end of the path, but before we could get there, Garon jumped out in front of us.

"Well well well, if it isn't my two favorite dragons." Garon said with an evil smile on his face. Just then, five more dragons came around the corner, each a different type, but all of them looking like they were up to no good. I was speechless. Our worst fears had come true, and we were literally at a dead end. I looked over at Dagger. He was trying his best to look tough, but even I could tell that it was just an act. I thought back to the scorch marks on the wall, and nearly trembled. Thankfully, I didn't though. In fact,

since I had nothing to lose, I decided to try something risky.

"Wow Garon, six of you? You're making this really unfair... for you!" I was bluffing, but hopefully, he'd take the bait. It was mine and

Dagger's only chance. Garon looked at me, and then over at Dagger. Thankfully, Dagger was now able to look confident. I think he knew what I was trying to do. As long as Garon thought we really were confident that we could beat his entire crew, we might actually be able to get out of their in one piece.

"Alright, I'll bite. I've partnered up with another team. There are six of us, which means we might as well be an army. Somehow, there's only the two of you, and I'm assuming that's because your partner knew better than to stick with a losing team, yet you still think you might get out of this... why?" Garon said, and I knew I had him hook line and sinker.

"It's simple. We found the mystery chest, the one with the secret weapon in it, and if you walk away now, then we won't follow you, and that's a promise." I lied. Garon was still smiling confidently, but I could see in his eyes that he was worried.

"No way, I don't believe you. What in the world is so powerful that you two twerps could defeat me, much less all of us?" Garon said. That confirmed it; Garon hadn't found the chest after all! If we could just get out of there, we'd still be able to find it, and then we'd be sure to win.

"Garon, we already defeated you once in the forest, what makes you think we can't do it again?" I asked, successfully getting under his skin. Apparently, Garon hadn't told his team mates about that, and they were starting to give him funny looks. I thought that's what I wanted that he would get shaken up and back down, but instead, Garon just got angrier.

"You know what? That was a fluke, and I promise you it will never happen again. And do you know what else, Morach? I think you're bluffing. Now get ready to say good bye to your shot at becoming the Ender dragon." Garon said, and he started walking towards Dagger and I. We backed up, but knew that the maze was against us. Eventually, we had our backs up against the wall, and Garon had his crew standing around him to watch him send us home. Dagger and I could have tried fighting back, and hey, we might have even been able to take out Garon. We might have even been able to take out of few of the other dragons. But we both knew it was hopeless, and that all of the dragons except for Garon didn't mean anything personal, they were just playing to win, and we couldn't blame them.

Dagger and I braced ourselves for a torrent of fire. Before it hit us, our health would go down to zero hearts, and we would be teleported back to the loser's area. Our shots at becoming the next Ender dragon would be gone forever. But then something amazing happened.

In a flash of green and blue, a mystery dragon ran by and rammed into one of the dragons on the right. Instantly the dragon disappeared in a puff of smoke, leaving behind the blue and green dragon. Garon and the rest of his team were shocked, so they all turned to launch the fireballs they had been planning to fire at us at the blue and green dragon. They all came together into one massive flaming ball of heat and light, surging forward at the dragon, but he just stood there, uncaring. When the fireball hit, the explosion shoot the entire maze to the point that Dagger lost his balance and fell down, and I had to hold on to the wall for support.

The blue and green dragon was not only still there, but he looked unhurt. Then, he lunged forward and took out three more of Garon's crew like it was child's play. I couldn't believe what I was seeing, and neither could Garon. In fact, Garon and his two remaining team members were already trying to make a getaway.

"Who even are you?" Garon shouted, running away at his top speed with his team trailing close behind him. The blue and green dragon turned, faced him and shouted.

"Leave my team mates alone!" he said, and then I realized who it was. It was Flip, and he had a full suit of diamond dragon armor.

"Flip? I thought you stole the apples and ditched us!" Dagger said. In response, Flip handed him three apples, and then tossed three apples my way. Without saying a word, he then turned and started walking. Dagger leaned over towards me while munching on a golden apple.

"Look, Flip's an odd fella, but he's the best shot we have at winning, we might as well all win together. I just hope he knows how to navigate as well as he can fight." Dagger said, and I had to

agree with him. Flip had proven himself to be loyal, so he deserved to be welcomed back in the group. Besides, we needed him a lot more than he needed us it seemed.

By that time, the sun was just peaking up over

the horizon, and none of us had gotten any sleep whatsoever. We decided that a nap was in order, and after explaining to Flip that leaving and not coming back for two days isn't good for the team, we settled down and closed out eyes at last.

Although the rest was good in the sense that it was peaceful, we most certainly didn't get enough of it. By noon, the sun was beating down on us and we couldn't sleep through its bright white light, so we had to get up and trudge along, following Flip and hoping he was leading us in the right direction.

After at least two hours of that, the sun was hanging lower in the sky, and we were beginning to get worried. The teacher had said that the gate would open at the end of day three for one hour only, and here we were, near the end of day three, and we still hadn't been able to find it.

Flip led us down yet another dead end, but this time, there was something there. It was a small gray button, attached to the wall, looking tantalizing. Dagger took the lead and then instantly slammed his tail against the button.

"Hey, wait, what if that's a trap? Why did you

just smack it?" I said, and then the floor started rumbling, but this time, it didn't stop.

"My bad!" Dagger shouted over the rumbling. Just then, the wall began to move to one side, until it slid all the way to reveal a large corridor. The rumbling then stopped. We stepped out into the corridor, and saw that the walls of both sides had been moved to the side. To our left was a large wall, and to our right was... the exit portal!

"Flip, you've led us to the exit portal, and we're the first ones here!" I said happily. Flip nodded, but then pointed over to an opened wall that was across from us and closer to the portal. A group of three people walked through. As I continued to look around, I saw that there were actually quite a few teams coming through the spaces in the walls, and then it hit me. This was the reason no one found the exit until now, it's because there was no path to the exit until the button was pressed! But if that's true, then that also revealed something about Flip.

"Flip, is this why you were leading us in circles that first day?" I asked. Flip simply turned towards me, shrugged his shoulders, and then

nodded. He must have known that he had solved the maze and found the exit, but that the walls were in the way.

All of the other teams started coming out into the middle ground. On the side closest the gate, there was a large gathering, and they forced every other team to go to the other side. I looked over at the top of the gate, and noticed a large number twenty in bold letters. I realized then what was going on.

Only twenty dragons would be able to move on to the next round, and the group closest to the gate was planning on blocking it off until the gate opened, and then they'd all rush in and we'd all be stuck with nothing. Apparently, Dagger was realizing this before I was.

Dagger started walking to the middle of the corridor. Flip and I had no choice but to follow him. When we got to the center of the large grounds, the doors that led back into the maze slammed shut. Apparently, we were the last dragons to enter. The gate corridor was, for all intents and purposes, an arena now, and we were right in the middle of two armies.

We were facing the gate, and the army in front of it started shifting left and right. There were twenty of them, and only about ten of everyone else, including us. I looked at the gate army and hoped that I wouldn't see him, but of course he was probably the mastermind behind the whole thing. Garon stepped forward to the front lines of his army and looked at me in particular with evil grin. He knew that he'd finally won. I tried my best to not show my disappointment. The Maze was supposed to thin out the group, and I thought that if I made it this far, I might have actually had a chance at winning, but of course, that wasn't the case. One thing that I did like was the fact that quite a few of Garon's pals couldn't help but stare at Flip. There was no doubt that they'd heard was he could do. Sadly, I didn't think it would be enough, and neither did they. It wasn't fear in their eyes that I saw. They were just deciding where to launch their fireballs first.

"There you are, Morach. I was worried that you wouldn't make it in time to see me and my army take the win, but it looks like you and the rest of your loser pals will have a front row seat." Garon said. His army started laughing a bit, but it quickly died down. Garon seemed to attract the worst type of dragon, the kind that joined the bullies because it was easier than fighting back. The thing Garon didn't realize was the fact that he didn't call Flip, Dagger and me out by name, so the seven dragons behind us were just as angry at his remark as we were. They started walking forward, and eventually joined us, forming a small group. I turned and looked at them, and they all had that same look of determination that I did. They turned to me and gave me a single nod of approval. We might not win, but it looked like we were going to fight. I looked up at the sky, and saw that the sun was already starting to fall. If we were going to do something, it would have to be now.

"You might have numbers, but we have fighters. It's time that you learned to stop picking on the little guys, because they might just surprise you!" I shouted. Instantly, dragons from both sides began rushing toward each other. I looked up just before the two small armies collided and saw what looked like a dozen suns, shining so bright that I had to squint. Just a fraction of a second later, I was locked in battle with a spider dragon. The fireballs rained down on both sides, and luckily most of our army was able to dodge. Garon's army wasn't so lucky.

There were so many of them grouped together that they couldn't get out of each other's way fast enough and were hit by the full force of our long range attack.

The spider dragon and I were both fighting tooth and nail. I kept trying to sneak my tail around and get surprise hit in, but the dragon's eight red eyes kept track of it at all times. We both stood up on our back legs and entered into a struggle. I finally was able to swing my tail in and knock him over, gaining the upper hand, but not before I noticed his mouth open and the fire build in the back of his throat. When he fell onto his back, I rolled to the side, and was just barely out of the reach of his fireball. I charged my own and launched it at the spider dragon, which was now scrambling to get up, and when I fired, it hit him head on. The dragon disappeared with the fireball, and then I was tackled from the side.

"You runts think just because you got a few cheap shots in that you're going to get a shot at being the Ender dragon? Keep dreaming!" Said the dragon and he clamped his claws down on my sides, locking me in place. He charged a fireball, and this time there was nothing I could do because he was too strong.

"Maybe we do!" Dagger shouted at he flung a creeper dragon by the tail towards the dragon on top of me. When they collided, the creeper dragon started to flash a bright while color.

Dagger didn't notice because he was reaching over to help me up, so I used my tail as a spring board and launched myself up, crashing into Dagger and sending us both flying away from the creeper. The other dragons stopped fighting long enough to dash away, and then the creeper dragon exploded, sending himself and the dragon that had me pinned to the loser's circle. This time it was my turn to help him up.

"Thanks for the save back there." I said. Dagger smiled at first, but then quickly frowned, and pushed me to the side. A large fireball slammed into Dagger, and he vanished with it. He sacrificed himself for me. I turned to see who had launched the blast, and then clinched my jaw in anger when I saw who it was.

"Oops, didn't mean to hit you friend there. Don't worry though, you'll be in the loser's circle with him soon enough!" Garon said, charging up another attack. He was on the far side of the battle; every single dragon left in the competition was between us. Garon's army had taken heavy losses, with only eight of them remaining, but we were in an even worse position. The only remaining dragon was Flip.

Flip was trying his best to fight them off, but they were getting bolder and bolder the longer the battle went on. I rushed to his side, but he knocked me back.

"Wait, Flip, what are you doing? I can help you fight, we can still win this!" I said, jumping up and running back towards him. Flip fired a blast into the crowd, and they all dodged in different directions. They were distracted enough that Flip was able to turn around.

"No, Morach. You can get through the gate, but I have to stay here and hold them off. There is no other way. Good luck." Flip said, giving me one last smile before turning back to the now reformed crowd. Flip had managed to take out one of them with his quick attack, but this time they were on their toes. Then, flip did something amazing.

Flip was a slime dragon, and until then, I had always thought that just meant he was green and, well, slimy. But oh no, it means so much more. Flip became perfectly still for a split moment, and then he started to shake. When it looked like he was about to fall apart, he did. Flip split in two, and then he split again, and again, until there were eight Flips, all of them a little smaller than the original, but all in all the same old creepy Flip.

I had to blink a few times to be sure that what I had seen actually happened, and I wasn't the only one. All eight remaining members of Garon's army had a look on their faces that you'd expect someone to have if they saw a talking sheep grow wings and fly away. If it wasn't so serious of a moment, I would have been rolling on the floor with laughter.

Each one of the Flips paired up with one of Garon's team mates. Somehow, when he split himself, he managed to keep the armor on each of his clones, so Flip was at least as strong as they were, even though splitting himself made him weaker. He charged at them, and they were forced to back up, terrified that if one Flip could take half of them out, then eight would be no contest. Eventually though, they started fighting back. They focused their fire on one Flip at a time, and managed to send one of him to the loser's circle before I could even start running up to help. Then, all of the Flips formed a ring around them all and started pushing them together. Eventually, they were trapped in a cage made of Flip.

On the other side of the crowd, however, was Garon. I had been so wrapped up in Flip's battle that I had forgotten he was still blocking my way to the gate. He had his head tilted back so far that the scales on the top of his head were touching his back, and even from where I was, the flame in the back of his throat was almost as bright as the sun. He had been charging his attack for the entire time! Garon couldn't speak, but he laughed for a moment, and then launched his attack.

At first, I thought that it had backfired because nothing came out after he launched it, but after a good three second delay, the fireball flew out through his hyper extended jaws, passed his razor sharp teeth, and then directly towards me. It was huge, bigger than any fireball I'd ever seen, and it was fast too. Not the faster than most, but fast enough that the gap between the

fireball and Flip's makeshift prison was closing all too fast. When the remainder of Garon's army realized that he was planning on taking them out along with me, they started fighting back with all their strength. Once Flip's hold broke, his clones started dissolving with every tail smack and quickly launched fireball until flip was completely gone. They were still too close together though, and Garon's fireball quickly vaporized the dragons towards the back, and would be on the rest of them too quickly for them to dodge, and also too quickly for me to dodge. There was only one way that I could save myself and not let Dagger or Flip's sacrifices are in vane; I had to fight fire with fire.

I focused all of my energy into my throat, and felt the heat build until my throat began to burn. By that time, all but two of Garon's former army was burnt up in the flames. I wasn't sure if I could even hold all the energy I was forcing into a single shot, much less launch it. My entire body began feeling weaker and weaker as I drained more and more of my energy into what would be the decider for the title of the Legendary Ender Dragon. The last two dragons were consumed by the fireball and transported to the loser's circle. I pushed the last of my energy into the shot and tried my best not to black out. I was pushing the limits of what my body could do, and I could have passed out at any moment from exhaustion. Fireballs were meant to be charged up slowly for a reason. I didn't even want to think about what would happen if I went unconscious with all that energy trapped in my body.

Finally, I leaned back, and then slung my neck forward, using gravity to launch the ball of flaming energy with as much force as I could muster. The light radiating off of it was so intense that I had to turn away to keep from going blind. When our attacks finally made contact, there was a boom so loud that I lost my hearing for a moment. It felt like the world was going in slow motion. The force of the explosion was so great that I started flying up and back, then smacked my head on the glass ceiling. The last thing I remember hearing before going unconscious was that the gate had finally opened.

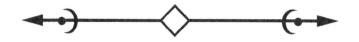

Chapter 5:

AND THE WINNER IS...

WHEN I FINALLY WOKE UP, THE FIRST PERSON I saw leaning over me was my teacher. She looked happy to see me. I sat up, and had two people come behind me and help me stand. I looked at both of them, and realized it was Flip and Dagger. They were both smiling as well. I looked around and saw a lot of familiar faces, all of them smiling. Then it hit me. I was in the loser's circle. Garon had won our duel. He was now the Legendary Ender Dragon.

I started feeling a bit dizzy at the thought of that, and needed Dagger and Flip to hold me steady. I was grateful for their help, but they were the last people I wanted to see. Being defeated in the first round of the Games wasn't all that bad, but coming in second after all the sacrifices my friends made to get me there was the most embarrassing thing I'd ever done. I couldn't look either of them in the eye, so I just stuck my tail between my legs and hung my head down in shame.

"I'm sorry you guys, I'm so sorry. You both had to give up your chances at victory just so I could go and screw things up like usual." I said, nearly tearing up. I didn't feel sorry for myself, but I did feel sorry for them. Dagger was a great person and a great friend, even if he wasn't that great of a fighter, and Flip was probably the best fighter out of anyone. He was a natural leader and always knew the right path, even when no one else did. All I'd done is stand up to a bully and then got knocked down in the dirt for my troubles.

"What are you talking about? You didn't screw anything up. We wouldn't have done it if we didn't believe in you. Besides, the person who won the title deserves it more than anyone else, that's why we have the Games." Dagger said. He approved of Garon being the Ender dragon, even after all that he'd done to him, to us?

"If you can know everything he did, and still think that Garon will make a good Ender dragon, then maybe he will surprise me." I said, trying to be optimistic, even though I wasn't.

"Wait... did you say Garon? No, Garon didn't win. He's not the Ender dragon, you are." Flip said. I looked in his eyes to see if he was playing a trick on me, but I could tell he was telling the truth. I had won.

"Wait, really? How?" I shouted, standing up straight. The teacher patted me on the back and then walked in front of me.

"Well, you both lost consciousness at the same time, and since you were the last two people and no one went through the gate, it was decided based on which one of you showed the most skill. You were both leaders in your own way, but Garon used fear to get others to follow him. He was manipulative and unkind. You, on the other hand, led with a much different approach. You didn't demand that you be the

center of everything. Instead, you led from behind the scenes and let your team mates use their individual skills to help the group. When you were faced with seemingly impossible challenges, you rose to them, and you were able to overcome them each time with your wit and your ability to inspire others. And after all was said and done, you had created such loyalty within your team that they were willing to give up their own goals in order to help you achieve yours, and then you went on to demonstrate that you realized that those were sacrifices that didn't have to be made, that they are not expected to make the sacrifices. All of those are the qualities of a great leader, and only a great leader can become the Ender dragon. Normally, we would see this develop over the course of the Games, but for the first time in the entire history of the Games, an Ender dragon was selected within the Maze. I am honored to be the first to properly congratulate you, Legendary Ender Dragon Morach." The teacher said. She then took a knee and bowed slightly. The crowd must have agreed with her, because they all repeated that same gesture then started cheering my name. Dagger and Flip were cheering the loudest and smiling the widest. In the very back of the crowd, leaning against a wall was Garon, smiling just barely, and clapping. We locked eyes for just a moment, and then he nodded. I nodded back. We weren't friends, but it was a start.

My name is Morach, and I am the Legendary Ender Dragon.

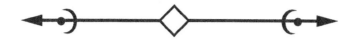

Chapter 6:

PORTAL PROBLEMS

STEVE COULDN'T HELP BUT TAKE A STEP BACK TO think about what he'd just read. The giant flying creature that he was must have been the Ender dragon... Morach. There was a whole dimension of those massive flying beasts, and yet they weren't actually beasts. They were as smart and kind as Steve had ever been. And somehow, someway, they were real! Steve knew immediately what he had to do, he had to find them, to talk with them... and yes, maybe have an epic battle or two. The world of Minecraft was suddenly bigger than it had ever been before.

Steve turned around, almost dizzy with

excitement about the prospect of a new adventure in a new dimension. There was a small wooden sign with an arrow printed on it. The arrow was pointed up a stair case, and Steve decided that this was the beginning of a whole new world. He made his way up the stairs, and was admittedly winded by the time he got to the top.

In front of him was something that he'd never seen before, and that was an impressive thing for sure. It was a large stone room. There was an arch to mark the entrance, and yet another set of stairs that led up to what must have been a portal, though it wasn't like a nether portal in the least. It was made of white and turquoise blocks, with strange designs on them. The whole thing was laying flat on its face. It was as if the Ender dragon had knocked it over as he flew back through. Lava cast a light glow on the bottom of the portal, and Steve realized that it hadn't been activated yet. He was mesmerized by the beauty of the thing, but was quickly drawn back to reality by the sound of a silverfish.

Ah yes, silverfish. Steve had a love hate relationship with the stone gray little critters. He

loved to take them out and hated to see them spawn. His first respawn happened because of an attack of silverfish. Steve decided it was time for a little pay back.

Steve pulled out his diamond sword and

started hacking and slashing at the mass of the creatures, taking two or three out with each swing of his blade. They would launch themselves at him, and he'd bash them back, but every time he took out five, ten more took their place. After keeping that up for a little while, Steve realized that there must have been a spawner somewhere in the room. Steve knocked a group of the little buggers away and then started dashing at the edges of the room, careful not to fall into the lava. The silverfish were quick, but luckily Steve was quicker, and before long he had a small conga line of them trailing behind him. Finally, Steve laid eyes on the spawner. A moment later he laid something else on it... the business end of his diamond pick ax, repeatedly and hard. In a matter of seconds, the spawner was almost ready to crumble to pieces, but not before the parade of silverfish were biting at his ankles like a pack of irritating puppies.

The spawner inevitably broke though, and then Steve pulled his sword back out and proceeded to play whack-a-mole with the remaining silverfish. A few minutes and thirty silverfish later, and Steve was now alone in the room with the portal glaring at him.

"Come on Morach, help me find you." Steve said. Looking around the room, there were no obvious clues as to how to get the portal to activate. With a nether portal, all you had to do was light the inside with a flint and steel and you were golden. It was an instant portal, just add fire. Steve decided it might be worth a shot, so he approached the portal and gave it a try; no dice. Of course all portals wouldn't be the same, that would make too much sense.

Steve started pacing around the room, getting more and more frustrated by the second. He walked over to the portal and tried throwing in or using everything he had in his inventory. He tried steak, cooked and raw, string, water, arrows, chicken, and apple, dirt, a single block of gravel, and finally, he tried repeating all of them but first he would say please. Apparently the portal didn't really care much about service with a smile.

Basically, Steve tried everything, and after trying everything, the only thing he wanted to do was nothing. Steve put everything away that he didn't accidentally drop in the lava, which was almost nothing, and plopped down, onto his back. He started looking up at the ceiling and wondering if Morach had really passed through there. Steve admired Morach because he was the hero that Steve had never had the chance to be. Steve had never had friends that he could fight for, or people that would sacrifice so much for him without wanting anything in return. Maybe that's why Steve was so board now that he'd maxed out in Minecraft. He didn't have anyone to share it with. While Steve laid there pondering that, he noticed something out of the corner of his eye. In the very corner of the ceiling, just above where the silverfish spawner had been, was a small chest embedded in the wall. The corners of the room were dark, so if you weren't looking right at it, you'd never see it. Morach hadn't let Steve down after all.

Steve used the last of his dirt and stone to build the ugliest looking staircase that had ever existed in Minecraft, ever. Steve would have time to sob over that later though, because when he opened the chest, there were two things. A stack of twelve black spheres called the eyes of Ender, and a note. Steve read it out loud.

"If you've made it this far, then I chose the right human. I've been watching you for longer than you might think, and I'm impressed. I want to meet you, and show you the world you saw small glimpses of in my book. Use these to activate the portal, and I'll see you on the other side, Steve. Signed, Morach." Steve thought he might faint. This was the invitation, and more importantly, the transportation he had been waiting for. Steve picked up all of the eyes of Ender and tucked away the note for safe keeping.

Steve then ran over to the portal and started carefully placing the eyes of Ender. Each time he placed one, the empty space was filled with a black swirling image that seemed to be almost alive. By the time Steve finished filling all the gaps and placed the last piece, the black portal looked... intimidating. The longer Steve stared at it, the more he wanted to just turn around and run away, but he didn't. Steve decided to take a note from Morach, and instead or running from

his fears, he decided to face them head on.

The moment of truth had come. Steve checked his inventory one last time, and made sure he had the essentials. He had a stack of steak, enough blocks to build a temporary shelter, and all the arrows he could shoot. Even though he'd been able to see the world through the eyes of Morach, there was no way to be sure what it would actually be like for a human in a world of dragons.

Steve could feel the weight of the Minecraft world on his shoulders. He had conquered dungeons, braved icy frozen tundra and dry barren deserts. He'd been in every biome and survived, come across dozens of strongholds, and built monuments and mansions that touched the clouds. He would be remembered in his world forever, even if there was no one there to remember it. Steve took one final deep breath and dove, falling head first right into his destiny.

End Vol. 1

I hope you enjoyed this *Amazing New Diary Of A Legendary Ender Dragon Adventure Series*. I hope you will take a moment and leave me a review. It tells me "we want more" and to keep writing these stories! It also helps others to find and experience these adventures and your reviews!

Make sure you check out my author page also! If you follow me there, you might just be our next random "Fan Fanatic Winner" for a FREE texture pack or character skin package! And receive our Minecraft Server URL! Or send us a <u>Video Review</u> of the your favorite Christopher Craft book and we will post it on our website!

ChristopherCraftBooks.com

THANKS A BUNCH! ... See you in Vol. 2!

Your Awesome!

Printed in Great Britain
by Amazon